The Baker
&
The Fox

Told by the Last Cookie - N - The Jar

By Michael Hill

To order additional copies of this book, contact:
Xlibris
844-714-8691
www.Xlibris.com
Orders@Xlibris.com

ISBN: Softcover   978-1-4257-0918-1

Print information available on the last page

Rev. date: 04/15/2024

The story of the Baker and the Fox is dedicated
to my beloved daughter La' Shawn

ч

Introduction

The Baker And The Fox is a one of a kind imaginary treat that will take you on a delightful journey. Never has there been a sugar filled quest that is not cavity forming, yet healthy for your imaginary system. Told by The Last Cookie – N – The Jar will bring to life in the fullest of beautiful colors that only your mind can bring forth. I hope that you enjoy reading it as much I did enjoy putting it together.

Michael Hill

6

Hello, my name is Oat and I'm an oatmeal cookie. I'm going to be your narrator through a fun and delightful story of how two became good friends; this is how it all happened.

Once upon a time there was a small town. To visit, people would travel from miles around. Everyone was happy. Especially, a Baker who's name was Happy Pappy.

Folk's would gather for a delicious sniff. That would leave their mouth watering from the very whiff. Without a single fuss, everyone would take time out for a bit of a delight, that was so grand and marvelous. Each and every bite was a sure treat that tasted just right. All in all it was a very filling event. It was indeed worth every cent. Everyday there was always endless smiles. People would happily travel from miles and miles. For some, as if just for the opportunity to get in on the wonderful smell, would attract costumers to come and say," Hello Happy Pappy", and sit for a spell. Each and everybody always as happy as can be. Enjoying Happy Pappy do his thing at the Bakery.

Day in and day out folk's would come by and say. "Hey there Happy Pappy, How are you doing today?" This time we've brought the rest of the family, to come and see you gracefully prepare your Danish with pride and care at your Bakery. And watch it bite  by bite disappear, with a nice cold glass of milk sitting right here.

One family said, "Your always so happy Pappy what is your secret?" Happy Pappy replied, " It's from all of the friendly smiles I get". Another family replied, "Wow, from all the tasty Pastries we can most certainly see how.

Now approached the time when another day had came to an end when it was time to say good- bye. That's when Happy Pappy said " This one is on me." And he gave everyone a big slice of pie.

All being so full could barely pull themselves to their feet to stand. Each and every one of them by Happy Pappy had to have a helping hand. All at the same time shaking their head, laughing they said. " Happy Pappy. To leave your Bakery always brings us to sorrow. So our dear friend when the sun comes up. We'll come again to visit tomorrow."

Now the very next day, folks set out to visit Happy Pappy in his Bakery from a mighty long way. The air was filled with the smell of fresh pastry and laughter, from the break of dawn there after. Soon as the sun came up. Happy Pappies Bakery had standing room only having everyone with fresh doughnuts and coffee in their cup.

Now there came up a gentle wind. As it blew... with the delicious smell of the bakery clear over the Meadows and Valley's it did send. To a tiny nose of a peculiar sly fox sporting a plaid suit and on its head a matching hat and bright red socks.

Yes the sly fox was something too see. But yet even more a sight once was hit by the delightful smell from Happy Pappy's Bakery. With the aroma of the tasty pastry smelling so fresh and sweet. Like a graceful Ballerina on the toes, there went the sly fox following the mouth-watering air over the Valleys and Meadows. Then as the wind died down. The sly fox found itself at the edge of town. As if from out of some sort of trance it woke...only to continue its quest following the Bakery smoke.

From watching through Happy Pappy's Bakery window, the sly fox looked at every table being filled.

The sly fox eyes grew three times bigger from looking at all the cakes, and pies.

The sly fox knew to get at all the goodies he had to get inside. Once there... to wait patiently until closing he had to find a place to hide. From the sly fox looking at the pastry started to become hard to hack. So he shifted his desperate location to see if there was a way around back. The sly fox was panicking, hoping that there would be a door opening. First, the sly fox went to the back door... but, it was locked and that passage wasn't available through that way any more.

Then the sly fox eye caught an open window way up high. So the sly fox thought he could go through the back bakeries window. But the sly fox was much too short so that mission he had to abort. He just didn't know how he could ever go through the much too high back Bakery window. So the sly fox went back up front, to see how he could possibly come up with another stunt. So, once to the front the sly fox arrived there. He just happened to see Happy Pappy's delivery driver unbuckle his belt from his truck chair. From the smell of the pastries, smelling so fresh and so warm, instantly gave the sly fox a brainstorm. The time has grown to be high noon. And as soon as Happy Pappy's driver made the delivery, the sly fox was free to the truck to go inside. There in a crate of delicious cherries he did seek a place to hide. So, as soon as Happy Pappy's driver came back for another load... Inside clear to the very back of Happy Pappy's Bakery, the crate of fresh cherries the sly fox too road. Trying to get those pastries

 was making the sly fox a hungry total mess. But little by little advancing to the pastries he was making progress. The sly fox begin to grin and smile, he knew it would be a short while, when he would be alone to dive into the Danish pile. But, when Happy Pappy came to the back of the Bakery to check his inventory he noticed the driver made the wrong delivery. So much for the sly fox luck. Back out with the crate of fresh cherries went him to the destination of the deliverer's truck. But, once back to the driver's truck inside, the sly fox, smooth as silk, was able to slip into and hide in a crate of fresh milk. So back in once again, this time sunk beneath a crate of fresh milk, the sly fox went, sniggling every passing moment. Without the slightest hesitation, once upon the fresh milk destination, the sly fox made a dash and jumped feet first into the trash. Then he took a sneak peak only a brief moment to stir, watching Happy Pappy gently placed the fresh milk in the refrigerator. From the sly fox new location, he could clearly see inside the entire Bakery and how it was so busy. Then came a gentle shout. It was the voice of Happy Pappy asking his driver to please to do him a favor and take the trash out. All the sly fox could do was stare, as with the can of trash he too went out the back door to be thrown in to the Bakeries dumpster. At being dumpster bound, the sly fox soon found himself upside down. There deep down in the dumpster, the sly fox sunk. He became completely covered in garbage that stunk. While holding it's nose, steadily watching the Bakeries back door close. The situation had really started to get to the sly fox. That was until he had seen the Mail Man go past the end of the ally and came up with a plan to mail himself to Happy Pappies Bakery in a special delivery box. The sly fox

14

managed to beat the Mail Man to his next pickup, which just so happen to be going to happy Pappy's Bakery that same day. Now the trip to Happy Pappy's Bakery shop was only the distance of a skip and a hop. Now the merchandise that was in the box was taken out and replaced with the sly fox.  Upon arrival Happy Pappy thought it ought to be his new bowls for his much loved dinner rolls. With out looking in the newly arrival box. That contained not the bowls for Happy Pappy's rolls but the sly fox. Happy Pappy politely asked the Mail Man if he could take it to the Bakery back. So the Mail Man did just that after letting down his mail sack. When the Mail Man placed the package on the table and then turned to leave. The sly fox was able to get out and squeeze under the table and crept over to the counter by where the cheesecake and the lemon moraine pie that has caught his eye. That just this morning, Happy Pappy did make. So the sly fox alone by himself with the opportunity to have anything he wanted on the shelf. At a split second of not thinking twice, the sly fox jumped out from under the table, and bumped his head on a near by big mixer, and was knocked out cold as ice. Just how much more could the poor sly fox stand, missing out on the opportunity to get at all the delicious cakes and pies, at hand. In deed it ought to have been a crime, missing what seems to be his last and final chance that time. So, the sly fox being unable, totally  asleep, slid softly and slowly back under the table. As the sly fox quietly slept, and slept, the precious time kept slipping fast away, to what for Happy Pappy and his costumers would be another beautiful day. Tick tock, tick tock, went Happy Pappy's Bakeries wall clock. All was well but not for the sly fox

who was sleep for a spell. And sleep he did, while in a curled up position made him hid. Mean while, the well-satisfied costumer's that was in Happy Pappy's front dining room all will be full, happy, and merrily on their way home soon. The time came with the sly fox peacefully asleep all the same. Now it was the time for Happy Pappy to clean up. But like every beautiful day, he gave everyone another slice of pie. And poured hot chocolate or coffee in all cups anyway. The Bakeries dining room, was filled with laughter and joy, and a good song together from every man, woman, girl and boy. The sly fox being asleep from being knocked out. He never knew, no... not one clue of all the fun that was going on in the Bakeries dining room.

Now the time came when it was getting down to their last bite. And some of Happy Pappy's customers had already gone home for the night. Left was just a few finishing what was left, and it became time to clean up. Though the tasty day again for Happy Pappy was fun. All in all it left for him a lot of work to be done. After all the fun was done and gone home everyone. Happy Pappy soon finished the front Bakery dining room. While wearing a smile on his face to attack was only left to be cleaned up was in the back. Now there in Happy Pappy's back Bakeries shop. After he had sweapted the entire room and had put up the broom and it was time to mop. While in the mop bucket the water was slowly pouring. A peaceful sound came around to Happy Pappy's ears to what sounded like a gentle snoring. Much to Happy Pappy's surprise he couldn't believe his very eyes. Happy Pappy had a big smile from ear to ear. Bending down gazing under the table there. Sleeping like a little pup. There snoring under the table was the sleeping sly fox in a ball all curled up. While moping passing

by the table Laughing quietly to himself. Accidentally Happy Pappy bumped into it then the sly fox woke. To the surprised sly fox Happy Pappy softly spoke. "My friend don't be afraid. I'm sure you must be hungry. Allow me to get you some cake, pastry, a bowl of fresh milk, or some fresh lemon aide." While partially sleepy the still curled up sly fox was watching Happy Pappy work so busy. Happy Pappy from the refrigerator bought forth cakes, pies, and cup cakes with chocolate dots for eyes. Banana splits made in the shape of boats. Happy Pappy even bought out assorted floats. It wasn't too long before the hungry sly fox was able. When him and Happy Pappy both sat and feasted at a very delicious full table. With the sly fox plate with cakes, pies, and cup cakes filled to the brim. Happy Pappy friendly asked the sly fox any time to feel free to stop by to visit him. So the sly fox did just that. Visited Happy Pappy at his bakery sporting his bright red sox with plaid suit and matching hat. Meanwhile, in Happy Pappy's kitchen was a dusty jar this is the story of the last cookie in the jar. The dusty jar was the only thing on a top shelf way up far. The cookie was made of chocolate dots imbedded in oatmeal. Once so very fresh, that's now hard as steal. It's been in that old glasses jar a long, long time that became very crusty. It had a lid on top of it that was the same way, and it was rusty. This is how the story goes. Told by the last cookie -n- the jar, the one who knows... It all started a long, very long time ago. When I was together with my friends in a roll of oatmeal dough. We had fun a whole lot. We even started smiling together as our faces formed dot by dot. It was neat. We were all

in array on a cookie sheet. It was a good feeling, we always sniggled at each other while looking up at the ceiling. On our backs we were laid. Only with the freshest of ingredients we were made. There wasn't a lot to do. We just waited around to be eaten up like people such as you. There wasn't too much time for each other to get attached. We knew the time we came out from the oven... one, two or a few of us probably would be snatched. I clearly remember a time, when a gingersnap cookie, a newly friend of mine. Barely from being sprinkled with sugar had time to cough, when he'd then been picked and his head broken off. Then in milk up and down dunked in a cup. He was repeatedly swished around then swallowed up. Another time a friendship of mine became undone. Do to a little boy who was the storeowner's son. He'd come running from behind a divider curtain, He'd snatched up a fortune cookie laying on him a real hurten. He didn't have a chance to say, what was inside his own fortune that day. My other strawberry cookie friend, the storeowner's son picked up and gave a hardy laugh. With his dirty grimy hands broke her in half. Then he'd played with her broken parts trying to match. Then my strawberry friend went down the hatch. Sadly to say that very same day, the storeowners son, picked up my other cookie friends and dropped one. I'd always thought that was a waste. No one would ever have an opportunity of his taste. From the storeowner's son, my cookie friend hadn't any more to fret. Once hitting the floor, he'd rolled through spider's webs under the cabinet. Time to time I could hear him say. "Hay. Even though under this cabinet is cold and lonely, I still wish I was ate up by

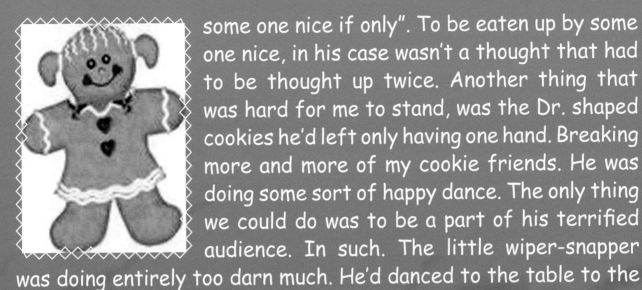

some one nice if only". To be eaten up by some one nice, in his case wasn't a thought that had to be thought up twice. Another thing that was hard for me to stand, was the Dr. shaped cookies he'd left only having one hand. Breaking more and more of my cookie friends. He was doing some sort of happy dance. The only thing we could do was to be a part of his terrified audience. In such. The little wiper-snapper was doing entirely too darn much. He'd danced to the table to the other side of the room. He'd picked up a cookie and bit off the bride from the groom. What was left was a mess. Even on his way out was a trail of what once was a beautiful ballerina who wore a beautiful dress. All we could do was horrifyingly glance. Then for our fallen cookie friends give a moment of silence. We were lucky, the ones he'd left. We'd had shook so much that some crumbs fell off; it had taken a while to catch our breath. It was sad; we couldn't do anything

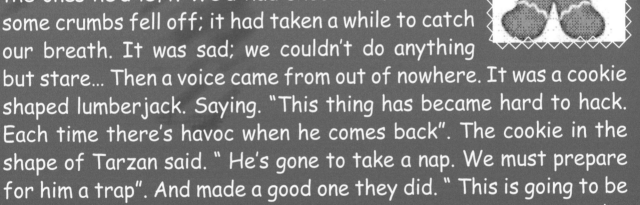

but stare... Then a voice came from out of nowhere. It was a cookie shaped lumberjack. Saying. "This thing has became hard to hack. Each time there's havoc when he comes back". The cookie in the shape of Tarzan said. " He's gone to take a nap. We must prepare for him a trap". And made a good one they did. " This is going to be fun". Laughing the cookie shaped kid. While sliding in on powder sugar, the cookie shaped Santa came. Chuckling all the way saying.

" We're going to put that little boy to shame". Then from off his back, the cookie shaped Santa quickly lowered his toy sack. He tied a rope around it then hung the sack over the entrance door. The cookie shaped G.I.Joes said. "Lets give him what for". The cookie shaped kitten with a

 long tail, knocked over a gallon of fresh milk into a pail. Then a cookie shaped little girl with the pail of fresh milk, climb upon a chair. Hung it on the doorknob, climbing down leaving it there. The final word was given. "Ready is the trap. Now we just wait till that little rascal comes back from his nap". It wasn't long, that a cookie shaped Gladiator struck his gong. For what had caught his eye, was a small but yet to them a giant figure that had darken up their light bulb sky. The cookies in the shapes of newborn babies sucking their tiny thumbs. All at the same time took them out whispering. "I see him, here he comes". The cookie shaped little girl standing next to the cookie shaped long tail cat, said... "He can come in if he wants too, but if I were him I wouldn't try that". No sooner then those chuckling words were said. There through the partially opened door, came the storeowner's son's head. The cookie in a shape of a strong man, rolled from off of the counter on top of the little boy a flower can. And clear from under the table  legs. The G.I. Joes Launched from measuring spoons fresh grade eggs. Then the cookie in the shape of a little boy, without saying a word, once cutting the rope was the loudest noise ever heard. It was the noise of fallen cookie shaped Santa toys. For what was all inside the sack, came thumping down on the little rascals back. Right after the store owner's son managed too scramble from out the room, the cookie shaped pirate gave out with a yell, "good  work me mates. He shouldn't be back no time soon". The cookie shaped little girl said. "Now, he should let us be". Then all the cookies at the some time said ... "Lets party". From that moment on, it was

24

 nothing but fun. All us cookies were having fun everywhere, even the cookies in the freezer. You could hear the laughter coming way from the back. It came from the cookies that had been boxed up and placed in a stack. Some cookies were having so much fun; jumping off from here and there didn't even notice they accidentally turned the oven on. For a few cookies that were playing in the oven, continued playing pretending they were strong. But their chocolate smiles started happily melting before very long. On the upper shelves were cookies of all sorts. From Santa Claws Whiskers, to food colored frogs with warts. There were cookies in the shapes of Gorillas and Apes. As well some were in assorted colors of a beautiful tropical shade. There was cookie shaped mermaid girls, sitting on big pretty ocean pearls. Even with them were some only having colored dots? And some in the shapes of brave Astronauts. Just a whole bunch of cookies. Such as cookies of Spaceships and rockets, even with various little boys having their hands in their pockets. And not too leave out those in shapes of shooting stars, and in the shapes of sport cars. Having their drivers face, in determination for first place. Yes! Those were the fun days. We were oblivious it wasn't going to last always. There were cookies in the shapes of pup, played so till some fell from the counter ending all broken up. Each and every night, the cookie shaped baby kitten would play fight. All around me was a variety; it was endless to sharing each other's company. When it came to fun, we didn't know the meaning of quit. With us cookies, that was the size of it. That was until… one of the playful cookie shaped puppies accidentally made a spill. For what was knocked over was oil - can, and down from the

 upper shelf it ran. The oil dripped to the stoves pilot light; upon contact, it started a fire and did ignite. Once the fire started, all memory of fun departed. The cookies in the shape of a King and Queen gave the command." We need help from every hand". The cookie shaped guards quickly went to their post. All around was yelling and screaming from cookies already in a roast. The fierce fire already out of control went higher and higher. The cookie shape strong man with his mighty arm broke the glass on the box to sound the alarm. From clear down the street there came running a stampede of feet. Meanwhile, for the cookies it was hard to hack, the fire grew bigger and bigger even though they fought back. It was a bitter cost; already to the furious fire a lot of cookies had been lost. Never ever around town has there been a fire such as this before. Never ever do anyone want to endure another such as this anymore. Higher and higher, the fierce fire in the cookie store rose, its heat was so intense that all the cookies in the freezer it melted there tiny gum drop nose. The fire brought sad attractions burning up what were once playful actions, though its fire ragged was soon to end. For help was coming around the bend. What seems for the cookies was the run out of luck, all changed with the sounds of a fire truck. The cookies gave a big shout, seeing the once fierce fire get distinguish out. But for the cookies the sadness was not yet done, if not by the fire. Water ruined everyone. That night for all in a city was a sad sight. Crying was on each and every shoulder, for what was left of the cookie store was only a smolder. Though the fire been out and all has gone home. There under the rubble was a cookie - n- the jar that was all alone. The poor cookie couldn't believe all his cookie

 friends were either washed away or fried; all during the rest of the night he cried. Come morning someone sadly said," What could have caused so much trouble, how could they do such a thing that would leave our cookie store such a rubble?" Someone said, "Maybe there was a theft, the culprit didn't want to leave any clues left." Just how the fire started no person in the city will ever know. To be the worst fire in the city... to history it will all go. This story told by the last cookie –n - the jar may seem to be mean...you can relax now for to him, it was all just a bad dream.

Printed in the United States
by Baker & Taylor Publisher Services